# Chocolate & Rose Pepper

*May 21, 2006*

Along the well worn verboten path
Amongst the safer russet roofs I fly
behind the dream

with broken promises

and tear stained face

I may be gone

But gone is not a place

never came to that, and today we're all laughing about it. And now live from the days of peace and love, and Rare Earth gives up a couple of their minutes because I went over two or three ~ I could never count and sing.

For a person in an audience I think it would be fun. For me... it's tricky, but it gives me this great opportunity (because it was so long ago and so many brain cells away) to sing other people's hits and pass them off as my own. Who will know? "Those were the days my friends, We thought they'd never end. We'd sing and dance forever and a day ....."

It's not the lineup of usual suspects. And then there is ME! But remember, there was a time, and this almost happened, when Jimi Hendrix would follow Joan Baez and Ravi Shankar (sitar player and father of Norah Jones) was before Melanie, and Sly and the Family Stone and Creedence Clearwater (one of my all time favorites) could all be seen at any time at any show. It was just all music. And when "There's only two kinds of music, good and bad." (I think it was Count Basie who said that) seemed to be the rule. When musicians transcended category, almost. Before the reins were pulled and the people began to buy into what the marketers were selling. "What do you study in school?" The answer eight out of ten times is "Marketing!" out, my dear ones ~ but you already are watching out, aren't you? Yeah, you're a pretty clever group.
Someday we'll all take over this planet and live happily ever after in the Motherhood of Love.

So back to Hippiefest and 25 minutes. There's a lot of musical integrity here, not just a bunch of musicians dressing up and being clowns ~ summoning up old images and stamping out performances. People are actually playing their music live, still. Rare Earth, Janis Ian, Felix, Leslie West, all falling out of the safety net, flitting, flying, and holding on tight to nothing at all. It's a beautiful circus. Where are the clowns? Not here. Except for Wavy Gravy, who introduced me and whispered in my ear something in Sanskrit. I think it means "May all the beings of all the planets be happy." I'm just guessing. It's the only thing I know in Sanskrit, and it is in my song to Amma. Phonetically, it sounds like this: Lokah Samasta Sukhino Bhavantu.

*__May all the beings of all the planets be happy.__*

# Death Runs in My Family

*February 3, 2007*

My Dear Ones,

Can you stand it ~ Momma's gotta talk.
What if something terrible does happen ~
I am putting that out there because I am leaving
the 50's and entering the 60's,
and I sort of wish I didn't have to know.
I don't care that you know, I just think it would have
been better if I didn't.
I know this isn't the voice of wisdom speaking, and
that these are other people's considerations, some
kind of "group think" that I would like to avoid, have
been living to avoid, "beat the system".

I have been 50-something for a long time and before that 40-something and so on.
And now SIXTY.
There is a little more anxiety with this next decade as we count down and watch the ball with
whoever, and pop that cork one more time.
You see, death runs in my family.

It used to be Guy Lombardo and couples dancing,
grownups wearing silly hats cheek to cheek and Auld Lang Syne,

blowing paper horns, and shaking tin rattles.
My grandmother and me, we banged pots and pans at the stroke of midnight.
My parents were out, maybe dancing with Guy Lombardo.
Something comforting about seeing the same old, Auld Lang Syne.
Then it was Dick Clark.
I sang on his TV show before he did New Year's Eves and replaced Guy Lombardo.

Now I am in a different time zone and it is confusing because it's really only the New Year, officially, when it happens in New York.
Even though it happens an hour later here, and you could say I am Sixty one hour earlier in New York when

I am really still 50-something here.
Maybe I'll just keep traveling west for a while till it all blows over.

Now this is just a suggestion, but if you want to get me something really nice,
I am still looking for a spot.
I'd really like it to be my own spot too. For the 3 day Melanie fest with:
Orchestra Night,
Roots/World Night
And then Rock out
"cause time's just a beat to a rock 'n roll heart", right?
Right.

# What's Good For You

*June 3, 2007*

I've been re-reading, and before that, burning my journal entries. Some just didn't seem right. Either the timing was wrong, or they just didn't ring true. True enough in the moment written, but then on re-read "which one of the Melanie's was that?" and should anyone be lured into spending any thought on her at all?

I have a little wood burning stove next to my primitive wooden desk. The desk is marked by years of being painted, stripped and in some spots sadly held together with an alloy metal nail from a grandfather or great-grandfather who didn't recognize the value of its pure primitive antiquity. There is a gouge on the right bottom corner that fascinated me as a child. Between the darkness, probably a burn hole, sanded out and the way the knots in the wood come out on top, it is a wolfie kind of bear monster... or my grandmother with a big hat. It was my grandmother's desk, and the only thing I have from her... so it's probably the latter. The wood stove I found at the Englishtown Flea Market in New Jersey about thirty years ago. And so now you have the picture. I write and write and then burn anything that falls short just in case any materials get into the wrong hands from the trash. I think there are people who on occasion sort through my trash. Every once in awhile someone brings something for me to sign, causing me to wonder... didn't I throw that away some time ago... so the stove is the better way. Now here we are, some that escaped the fire:

47

## My Dear Ones,

I'm getting more back by the day and far away is looking farther away as I chew each bite thirty times, or at least very well... before taking another. There are things in this life that are good for you. Those things vary immensely from person to person. For instance, I heard Sting say he plays jazz because he feels it is good for you. Perfect example I think. Jazz isn't good for me ~ but chewing raw bits very well is. Maybe Sting agrees. So here I am, back and not so far away chewing something called "energy soup". I believe Dr. Ann Wigmore invented it and I've had many variations. The final result is always green and pulverized and you chew it although there is very little to chew. The ingredients put me in the mind of the old Saturday Night Live Bass-O-Matic skit. Into the Bass-O-Matic goes -- say...

Dulse

Watermelon
Sunflower Sprouts
Organic Baby Greens
Raw Spinach
A few Soaked Almonds
2-3 Dried Figs

You turn on the Bass-O-Matic, pour it into a bowl, top it off with your choice of slivered apple, figs, avocado or banana.

Just a bit now...it's not a fruit salad! This is breakfast, lunch and dinner with mid-morning veggie juice.

Yeah, I'm back with Brenda Lee. Dia tells me she's on some sort of juice fast too. I'm sure Howard isn't. Howard is seven feet tall...or more...has a quick smile, and everything he does, including raising monster Spanish mastiffs and doing sound all over the world (Dubai was in-between the Queen of The Netherlands and me) is good for Howard.

Some people are like that. I think Christiane Amanpour must be like that. Sting and I are not. He plays jazz...I chew green liquid slowly.

Some people are just lucky I guess. Before I came back to Brenda Lee's I wrote a song with Grammy Award Winner Kim Williams...it was a thrill. Kim Williams has written at least eighty hit songs. He doesn't miss ~ I miss a lot. We go at it from very different approaches. Me...willy nilly... meandering, and then "ooh, I like this"... I can land here and pursue. Oh yes, this is...and here we have the crux of it...THIS IS ME. Why is "me" so important? It's the one I've spent a lifetime studying. Partly, to get along with you...and partly because life is pretty funny and temporary and not altogether clear...and here I am with a body, mind and soul.

There are so many things out there to learn, but whatever they are still get translated by my universe... like it or not. So I better figure out as much of what is my universe so I can know what to do about what's out there.

The possibility that it doesn't matter is not a possibility in my universe. I guess that's one example of meandering. After our writing session we all went out and ate a steak...nearly raw for me...and chewed very well. But not as well as when I'm eating energy soup ~ go figure.

My dear ones ~ never say never and chew well. Promise?

Who knows what's good for you...

# Maine

*July 26, 2007*

## My Dear Ones,

For a short while this summer I lived in Maine. I must have grown up there in another life. I have fond memories of blueberry picking, hopping rocks, and clam mud squishing through my toes. But in this life, I'm from "away," which is the most perfect description in a word ~ an applicable explanation of why. Why no matter where I've lived or go, someone will say, "you're not from around here, are you?" "No," is my reply. And if I had known then what people from Maine, I mean really, as in generations, think I would have replied, "no, I'm from away," and let it go at that, rather than give that sometimes long list of where I am from.

### The list:
Born in New York, uptown and down ~ Queens (Bayside/Flushing/Astoria),
then New Jersey (South like Bruce)
back to the city, New York City,
back to New Jersey (South) ~
and then the big leap
London, England
Paris, France
Amsterdam,
The
Netherlands
Austria (near
Innsbruck)
Germany
(near
Munich)
back to
New York
City
New Jersey
(South again as in
Bruce)
Florida (West Coast, not as in Palm Beach
where they didn't know how to vote)

The Netherlands (Ilpendam)
to Tennessee (as in Davy Crockett) where I wasn't born on a mountain top,
and am certainly from "away."

In Maine, if you're not really (generations) from Maine, you're from away. Even thirty years, one artist told me. (Gail Page, who wrote a beautiful children's book How to Be a Good Dog, you need to get it for every child or the child in anyone who loves dogs.) Even if you're there fifty years, and raise children there, your children are still from away. It's been said if you put kittens in the oven, you don't get muffins, they're still from away.

I hold onto details like this. I'm a refugee like my grandparents. I remember their memories.

I don't regret this, it's just that if I grew up in Maine, I could remember my Uncle coming to get me to go out and set the Lobster traps ~ getting the bait, eating a donut, and drinking coffee, even though I'm too young to drink coffee, they put a lot of milk in it for me. I'd be able to remember January and February and believing the whole world lived in winter forever, the roads flooding over in spring, and mud. Mud was invented in Maine. Houses wouldn't have mud rooms if it weren't for Maine ~ but I'm from away.

I was gone then, I was in New York, remembering picking wildflowers and blueberries in Maine in another life in Maine. But there were dandelions in the park, or sometimes those very delicate weed flowers that were a pale periwinkle blue, maybe you know, I never knew their name. They grew around a square of earth where the building superintendent grew a fig tree. It was magic. He wrapped it for warmth in the winter, unwrapped it in spring, and in summer cut off figs. He was Italian and made wine in the basement. The pungent smell of fermentation and pungent basement and Italian super, are mingling with the scent of clam mud. He is the only super I remember, he brought his little Italian universe to 2312 31st avenue and shared it with me, a girl from somewhere else. We were both from away. "I'll drink some of yours if you'll drink some of mine, cause I can't stand the taste of leftover wine." The scent of musty basement wine lingers in that song.

Sal Detroia has passed away while I was living in Maine and it isn't real that he's gone. Gone is not a place. People can't be gone. He's right there in the studio with me, we're recording my songs in A minor and E minor because Sal is the unquestionable king of nylon guitar for recording sessions in New York in the sixties. My first encounter was on "Beautiful People" in C. It was so difficult for me to translate to musicians what I heard in my head, not having studied music. Three chords on the guitar, no theory, no terms ~ you can't hum a chord, you can only hum one note at a time, one of the shortcomings of the voice. The head has a whole chord, the voice comes out as one note. I would try to communicate with trained musicians and this is where Sal came to my rescue, he heard the chord in my head and became a friend for life. He played and created the intro to Simon and Garfunkel's

"The Boxer." And needed to get acknowledged for that as so many musicians who create the memorable hooks and riffs do. But no one told the world it was Sal Detroia ~ Sal, anyone who matters knows, mostly you, and you know, and you'll carry that beauty through from life to life because gone is not a place. And I will not miss you because you'll always be right there.

My dear ones it's been almost a month in Maine and soon I'll be remembering growing up or raising my children in other places, anywhere but gone.

P.S. The privacy laws are strictly upheld here, I will only say I am the lucky guest of Dick and Jane. They lived in this cottage before they built their dream house down the hill. We are on the water, I think all of Maine is on the water, but this is a most prized safe harbor. There have been times (don't hate me) when my happiness for others having happiness has been ruined by my longing for what they have, it's the lowest of human conditions, but in all fairness to me, sometimes what people have is use as a weapon and one of the bad human defenses is envy. Here, there is spirit. I have to end that sentence because it would run on and on. I need to say kindness, openness, generosity ~ benevolence, all surrounded by this beauty which was offered to me.

Knowing people like this exist, keeps me keeping my promise. I am surrounded by love and I cannot

 thank them enough for the songs I wrote in Maine in this house looking out at the water and sometimes not seeing it through the fog. Boats and clouds ~ for "how I spent my summer vacation" ~ and the books ~ angels, there are certainly angels I have a feather to prove it ~ foghorns ~ water water everywhere ~ Beau Jarred up to his neck in clam mud photographing sunsets ~ Elizabeth Tuttle who takes photos with an eighteen hundreds type camera under a black cloth and processing them on platinum ~ and Sarah who makes boxes with grasses and shells ~ and Annette who sells gifts and Lobsters (Jane said everyone here has two or three jobs) ~ the singer Jennifer Buffington who didn't make the finals on American Idol, which I think is to her credit, but she'll try again, she says ~ and Paul Noel Stookey from PP&M who was hiding from me ~ Paul Sullivan Grammy Award winner who was at the party ~ and Robert who paints "Americans Who Tell the Truth" ~ and Judith who gave us one of the best days of our lives ~ and all of you with two and three jobs ~ remember me from Away.

My Dear Ones, sometimes you're not in a position to write ~

As you might not know, since May, I've done concerts in Korea, a tour in England and a Hippiefest tour in the United States. I decided not to go straight home, but back to Florida and soak in the Gulf of Mexico and get healthy, as I was experiencing
symptoms of otherwise.

I have this idea for a musical, taking place in a mall sprawl with "Bed, Bath and Further than That" being implied with halo-ish magenta glow as a spiritual mecca. Where people celebrate the whoosh of Christmahanavaloween, beginning right after Labor Day. And in the middle of this superficial banality, a woman is contacted by an angel and told she has seven days to save the planet, and just when we thought that was what the Hard Rock Cafe would do. She is an unlikely candidate, an American modern-day "Juliet of the Spirits". I have the songs, but I don't want to ruin the end by telling ~ so I'm soaking and working and in-between I went to Mascoutah, Illinois. At one time the center of the population of the US. It's one of those places where I wished I might have raised my three children. It was all
because of Jeanne Bullard who was persistent, I mean, would not give up on her idea of Melanie singing at the Espenschied Chapel in Mascoutah. Sheer will with good intent really works, because I don't know how I got from my Gulf of Mexico hot tub to Mascoutah, the not-so-center-of-the-population-anymore chapel. But there I was being hosted by John Bailey, who has donated wonderful bronze statues of creatures and people in unlikely places all over town. The overall effect is almost startling, and for this reason, and for the Bavarian RoemerTopf Restaurant, Tony's Place, and Flowers, Balloons, Etc. antique store...you need to get off the main road and visit Mascoutah, Illinois and vicinity.

I know you weren't there when I was. It was homecoming night and there were thousands of cars at the high school. The chapel was right behind it, and for a minute I thought I was drawing record crowds, but soon realized that the chapel next to the cemetery was for me and the few others who could find it. If the bronze statues and all aren't enough, there isn't a Wal-Mart nearby. It's hard to find places like that, and if you know any, tell me.

But it was a warm cuddly night with the ladies (all volunteers) selling homemade cake at intermission and the constant wild cheering next door. Was it for me? Am I the homecoming queen? Our small but dedicated group really listened. And that is the important part. I did two shows. On Saturday I had the best Ice Cream at Dr. Jazz and girls were there in fancy dresses, and they were... well, there was kindness emanating from their tables. And good will even. No Disney Channel cynical girls, but nice people. Homecoming queens all. Genuine is the word that comes to my mind. Groups of girls and guys that in most places might provoke sneers and snides toward someone like me and my entourage.

And now my hero has seven days to save the planet, and I count on the people of Mascoutah to help as I go back to it and get ready for some shows in The Netherlands, my other hometown somewhere beyond the sea.

# Mozart

*August 16, 2007*

Man's best friend 15 or so
Hardly a life
For a dog it's old
Man's best friend born to be gone
Funk and fuzz dog years and bones
And the man goes home alone

Man's best friend's nobility
Was known to very few and me
I used to listen to his eyes
That held great wisdom and advice
Buried bones we'll never find
Funk and fuzz dog years and bones
And the man walks home alone

Often I was a child at his side
Let's go seek, let's go hide
Run and don't forget to play
The man walks slow for home today
Man's best friend born to be gone
Funk and fuzz dog years and bones
The man walks home alone

# Happy Christmahanavaloween!

*October 31, 2007*

Yay, hooray and Happy Christmahanavaloween! to you my dear ones,

The gift dealers can't wait to get that buying frenzy on fast enough. The jack-o-lantern is propped up as a snowman's head. It's one whoosh of holiday, so why not call it Christmahanavaloween.

Here is my song to help us celebrate the holidaze season. It even has its own address. christmahanavaloween.com. Try it out and share with friends!

Happy Christmahanavaloween
When labor day is over it begins
One greeting card to cover
everything
Confusing yes, no one will guess
We left out Kwanzaa

Christmahanavaloween, it stirs
Accounts are overdrawn as seasons
blur
Swear your love in chocolate things
Just buy it
After this is over we are going on a diet

Brotherhood and love and candy corn
Santa drank a Coke when Christ was born
Some good must come from all this effort, surely
The malls are packed
We're back in black
Does anyone get what they really wanted

Happy Christmahanavaloween
One greeting card to cover everything
Happy Christmahanavaloween
Happy Christmahana
Lets go shopping mama
Happy Christmahanavaloween

# Clean Towels

*December 19, 2007*

It's really countdown now, the 19th I think and I've just checked into the hotel. Washing my hands and "little things" and there it is, the sign dangling from the towel bar with the image of the one last drop of water on the planet and asking me to help conserve it by thinking hard should the towel be reused and hung back up, or should I be reckless to all mankind and throw it on the floor? I've just left a place where they were watering a corporate office lawn in the rain-I don't want to reuse the towel-first of all, I share a room with him and though he's clean, maybe that was his and I want a new one. Secondly, I am not sure about the towel to begin with. Who put them there, what were they touching before my towels and did they have a cold? ACHOO! "God bless you," I say and pick up a new towel. It is one of the perks of staying in a hotel and it is Christmas and I don't want to be away from home. I wrap myself in clean towels - sheets can stay on the beds for days, after all I've had a bath before bed and I'm not thinking about the who touched them part. I'm scrubbed, dried with a clean towel..."What do you want for Christmas, Melanie?"
"Clean towels." And I coast along awakeness into a solid doze.

A closer than inside my ear kind of sound rouses me. And the three articles of clothing, all black, two long, one short, are hanging from an impromptu clothes hanger made out of a ceiling lamp, looking very much to my drowsy eyes like three members of the Greek chorus on a break exhausted from Greek chorus work. I've hung them on hangers, yes, I am in a hotel that has hangers that remove from the closet pole, like the ones from home-another perk. So many road places have the kind that is a little ball contraption that fits into a metal ring, permanently attached. So you can remove the hanger but have lost the ability to hang it anywhere but back onto the hotel closet pole, preventing, I suppose, the thieving of hangers. Hangers!? I improvise so much in hotels and I love having removable hangers and I know that I might have upset some of you by poking fun at the environmental consciousness awareness last drop of water picture but take it in the spirit intended and someone tell them to stop watering the golf course in the rain.

Singing for me is mostly natural. Christmas songs, that come but once a year take some time to warm up to. I know the first line or two, then realize I don't know the song. Why not, you sang it last year? "Exactly." I'm going to do a Christmas show with friends and family. This brings to mind the image of twenty people on stage dressed in Victorian or fifties wear, like hats and muffs, bustling to and fro. A tree on stage, presents, some comedic schtick, some rehearsed patter. I don't have friends. I was thinking as I saw a magazine cover, "Stroll The Historic Sidewalks of the Capital Region," with a photo of these women dressed right, hats, long dresses.... THEY could be my friends! I wonder what they are all doing tomorrow night after the holiday stroll? Maybe they could stroll onto my stage and be the friends. I wonder if they like to bustle. Family-family is harder. I have three children. Two will be performing with me, Leilah and Beau Jarred. Jeordie is, um-coming home Christmas Eve. She could not be there but even so, three singers, two guitars, I worry. MELANIE, FRIENDS AND FAMILY, we're small but mighty. It's just the picture in my head as I imagine myself in the audience waiting for Christmas

with MELANIE, FRIENDS AND FAMILY,
munchkins, trolls, children, dogs, cats, monkeys, unicorns, the fringe element and
then WE appear, Beau, me and Leilah. No tree, no fireplace, no Grandpa, no Grandma, no kids, no
monkeys. Will I be okay? I'm thirsty. I only have one bottle of water, uh oh, one last drop. I sing O
Come All Ye Faithful in my head, tidings of comfort and joy and unto certain shepherds. Certain
shepherds are referred to in several traditional Christmas carols. I can't help wonder if there was an
elitist shepherd group or a secret society of shepherds who were posted to receive signals from
intergalactic sources to then interpret and signal other elitist shepherds and so on. A network of
shepherds, why certain ones, I wonder.

Well, I want to thank you all for allowing these ramblings over the years -there's really no one else like
you and at Christmas time, I wish to give everyone a gift. I've been looking in my travels for the perfect
thing. Chocolate is always right, but some can't and most shouldn't. Then I thought fire opals. Feels to
me what we all need right now but then again I could be wrong. Maybe amethyst, or tourmaline, garnets
or aquamarines, sapphires, just beautiful nine millimeter or so stones. I would pick out each one, not in a
setting, not jewelry store treated stones but in their more natural state, a perfect little jewel for
everyone. Right about here, the accountant goes mad. Even I was thinking, I might be low on funds. It
seems what I can give you is songs -they are still coming and ramblings from the Roadburn Cafe.
Someday I'd like to open a little place called the "Roadburn Cafe."We can go for coffee or depending on
what part of a cleanse I'm on, herb tea. Right now, it would be coffee or hot chocolate which reminds
me of the POLAR EXPRESS ~"because the bell still rings for me".

My dear ones, I love you all desperately. Happy Christmahanavaloween, Merry Christmas, Peace, Love,
Plenty of clear water and clean towels in the New Year.

# Looking Out

*April 3, 2008*

My Dear Ones,

Is this a book? Anyone out there want the book? Do you want to hear about Clive Davis, Bob Dylan, the life of an introvert in an extrovert world? How I wanted to be Joan Baez when I was in my teens, and how I adore her still? How about Judy Collins, or Joni Mitchell? My memories, subjective and mostly altered. Or should we just cut to the quick because, we are here now? My life, my life, the story of my life is much too long and complicated and most of it untrue.

People are very imaginative with their past. Hillary, you ducked sniper fire?

Well, I probably did too, were I allowed to write the book. Fortunately it's just me from the Roadburn Cafe in the here and now. My Dear Ones, can you stand it, momma's got to talk...

I've been off the road since New Year's and I am going to be in the UK soon. When I don't play out for awhile, I truly feel like I'm coming back from retirement. Do I still know how to do this? To make it worse, I got a funky flu - compliments of the funky flu planes over the state of Tennessee. Pharmaceutical flu planes spraying everyone down here with funky flu so they have to go get their funky flu medicine. But of course I'm mad. Don't pay any attention to me at all. Here's my disclaimer: "The opinions expressed here are the sole opinions of a raver who knows nothing".

So I'm going back to England. I'll pack my bag one more time and leave everything I love or hate ~ depart and arrive. I won't say I'm looking forward to getting up in front of a lot of people. They're all looking at me, maybe wondering if I can do this. Do I still know how to be beautiful ~ charming ~ daring ~ can I still sing, that's important. Singing well by my own standards, that is everything as it should be. But in the upside down world, where right is wrong, etc. some forget about the music, or the script, the singers, or the actors being good. Being great equates in this upside down world to how many times you've seen a person's face in the media, or heard their name. People being famous for being famous. And not so much, or at all in some instances, for what they do... With me, my voice opens a channel in my soul. It's good for me to sing. It's also good for the atmosphere. This is anything but scientific. But when I'm right on, a frequency, a vibration radiates from me throughout, can reach to the end of the hall or outside, goes skyward and creates this dome of clear beauty. And you're all in it. So you see, the love that radiates. It's what carries on and propels upward and onward ~ God, I can't wait to get to England!

# Leaving Godzilla Mountain

*May 5, 2008*

ey really love orange here. Even in the rest stop (which really
sn't an official rest stop, there aren't any). It was several
staurants strip mall style next to the tire sales and the fish
rket and twenty feet from an architectural modern-designed
autiful home along the well traveled road to the Demilitarized
ne, there were amazing brilliant sunburst glazed tiles in the
lway toilets. I'm sorry about the run-on sentences. Sure I
uld have broken it up and said it in other ways so you didn't
ve to read it again, but it's my style, which I cling to, and I
e the idea of you reading it twice.

le is like a body. You have everything before you are even
rn, and after you even die. But then you need this body to get
ound, etc. And then all the deviations and craziness and man's
umanity to man begin. I can almost remember being an idea
d flying, but tonight my body goes onstage at one of the
gest arenas in the world.

I have a lot of anxiety about doing this stadium tonight. The Olympic Stadium, left from the Olympics held in Seoul Korea in 1988, a very proud moment for Koreans, commemorated in souvenir shops and markers everywhere. Koreans are very proud and resilient. In ways, the people remind me of the Irish. They love to joke around, great sense of humor, and they like to drink up. Soju is what to have, a Shnappsie Sake ~ strong. And you can drink a lot without a hangover. Ahem, yes I know, and I can tell you, I love to drink, but this body thing ~ it experiences the results of too much alcohol poorly. I used to be able to drink a lot more, have fun, get naked, dance on tables, but now ~ I fall asleep without the nudity or dancing ~ oh, don't be silly, of course I never did those things ~ got naked, drank too much, danced on tables, threw up hugging toilet bowls, swearing "I'll never do this again," having to pack to leave for parts unknown with the room spinning

wondering why... "why me." No, none of that, and if I did, I don't remember. Just bits and pieces. I knew someone who always said, in 50 years it won't matter. "My life, my life, the story of my life is much too long and complicated, and most of it untrue."

Tomorrow my dear ones I will be leaving Korea. Mountains in the middle of skyscrapers. You half expect Godzilla to poke his head up and tromp through the city, devouring or clumsily stepping on cars, folks, Samsung, giant TV screens, buildings of western color. Taupe, white, grey, which obscure but

don't deny the greens and purples of a beautiful old culture of art and poetry, "beautiful sadness", Confucius, the missionaries who left behind neon crosses on top of the so many churches and leaving the heart and soul of this wonderful Korean culture. Goodbye Godzilla Mountain.

"The saddest thing under the sun above is to say goodbye to the ones you love"

Next time I hope I'll be able to go north, way north, which is cut off from the south. If I can't go in body, I send my voice. As a recipient of an honorary Ambassador of Peace award, my voice will carry north and the frequencies will tear down the walls and "the world will live as one - J.L."

This is my goal from one body to the next, silly girl ~

# Bed, Bath and Further Than That

*October 3, 2008*

My Dear Ones, sometimes you're not in a position to write ~

As you might not know, since May, I've done concerts in Korea, a tour in England and a Hippiefest tour in the United States. I decided not to go straight home, but back to Florida and soak in the Gulf of Mexico and get healthy, as I was experiencing symptoms of otherwise.

I have this idea for a musical, taking place in a mall sprawl with "Bed, Bath and Further than That" being implied with halo-ish magenta glow as a spiritual mecca. Where people celebrate the whoosh of Christmahanavaloween, beginning right after Labor Day. And in the middle of this superficial banality, a woman is contacted by an angel and told she has seven days to save the planet, and just when we thought that was what the Hard Rock Cafe would do. She is an unlikely candidate, an American modern-day "Juliet of the Spirits". I have the songs, but I don't want to ruin the end by telling ~ so I'm soaking and working and in-between I went to Mascoutah, Illinois. At one time the center of the population of the US. It's one of those places I wished I might have raised my three children. It was all because of Jeanne Bullard who was persistent, I mean, would not give up on her idea of Melanie singing at the Espenschied Chapel in Mascoutah. Sheer will with good intent really works, because I don't know how I got from my Gulf of Mexico hot tub to Mascoutah, the not-so-center-of-the-population-anymore chapel. But there I was being hosted by John Bailey, who has donated wonderful bronze statues of creatures and people in unlikely places all over town. The overall effect is almost startling, and for this reason, and for the Bavarian RoemerTopf Restaurant, Tony's Place, and Flowers, Balloons, Etc. antique store... you need to get off the main road and visit Mascoutah Illinois and vicinity.

I know you weren't there when I was. It was homecoming night and there were thousands of cars at the high school. The chapel was right behind it, and for a minute I thought I was drawing record crowds, but soon realized that the chapel next to the cemetery was for me and the few others who could find it. If the bronze statues and all aren't enough, there isn't a Wal-Mart nearby. It's hard to find places like that, and if you know any, tell me.

But it was a warm cuddly night with the ladies (all volunteers) selling homemade cake at intermission and the constant wild cheering next door. Was it for me? Am I the homecoming queen? Our small but dedicated group really listened. And that is the important part. I did two shows. On Saturday I had the best Ice Cream at Dr. Jazz and girls were there in fancy dresses, and they were... well, there was kindness emanating from their tables. And good will even. No Disney Channel cynical girls, but nice people. Homecoming queens all. Genuine is the word that comes to my mind. Groups of girls and guys that in most places might have been provoked to sneer and snide toward someone like me and my entourage.

And now my hero has seven days to save the planet, and I count on the people of Mascoutah to help as I go back to it and get ready for some shows in The Netherlands, my other hometown somewhere beyond the sea.

# A Lie by Omission

*May 8, 2010*

My Dear ones, I'm here in Nashville.

The blackout in New York in '68 I think, Woodstock, you know the one, people coming together in unexpected numbers. Hurricanes in Florida, and now the Nashville flood. That amazing caring, sharing, camaraderie that overtakes people in disaster seemingly dormant till such time.

I've never sensed or been among such a group of dedicated humanists in my 63 or so years of living. With lost lives, missing people, horrific stories of life and death struggles and survival. Lost history, thousands of families without the home they left that morning, schools, some barely surviving before, and now? And now.

Just now, one whole week later our national government has just sent someone, not exactly president or vice president or Hillary, but someone of not so high visibility to assess the damage. Obama did call Brad Paisley and said to him "save my Opry". Now I find the people without media coverage, without too much meddling have done MORE. Tennessee is perhaps ironically or aptly called the volunteer state. I hardly feel qualified to write from where I sit on this glorious southern sunshine day. Nothing has happened. From this vantage point, the lake is just a bit muddier. This looks like what the Washington/Media people want us to see. But one mile down the street? Disaster. The nature of flash flooding rivers. Rivers, major rivers. Damns on the verge of compromise, and no coverage! Where are those helicopters that circle over the floods in the Midwest where only farmland was underwater. Not landmarks, history and people.

And this is my take. Aside from Anderson Cooper and we thank you for that, I'm sure you'll get some flack for it. The media and Washington have ignored, for the most part, what has happened, and is happening here. Yet, people rose to the cause with or without them. This is my point through all this rambling.

Meddling ~ people do best with less.

Money is good, blankets and food, but meddling? people do best with less.

# Oh God I Love People

*May 29, 2010*

So My Dear Ones,

Life goes on ~ without being sappy, I will just say that the people here are to be highly commended for their actions taken to help neighbors or in so many cases, complete strangers.

I am moved beyond words. They took action without credit, attention, votes or getting anything in return. Oh God, I love people, and how mostly they're so good. Well, they keep dogs and cats don't they? Isn't that proof? We are however in a place and time in this world where politics/media are dangerously powerful in that their influence is being exerted on us. Lots of people are actually afraid to think. Especially out loud because they might look as if they are one of those, or worse, one of "those". I suspect the real thinkers are going underground, so to speak. We live in an age of marketing and categories. We must rise above categories. We're humans with imaginations, whims, thoughts of endless possibilities and so on.

For those who might wonder, when I return from England's Isle of Wight festival and all that goes with it, I'm planning a concert series. Neighbors helping neighbors. Grassroots. As little in "organization" as possible, one on one. I'm doing my first for a family. An artist I know who lost all his ways of making a living. Instruments, computers, of course everything else. His wife and child managed to get out at 5 AM , rescued by a friend's canoe. So all the proceeds will go to Tony and family to help rebuild their life.

I've been involved in so many charities and supposed not for profit efforts where the amounts raised don't exactly go to those wonderful humans I spoke of previously. So the idea is, one family at a time. Raise money to help them rebuild. At the end of the show, the audience will be told how much they raised for the family. Of course Beau and I will donate our time and performance without the need to recover expenses because we live here. What I'm hoping is that other artists take this idea and run with it. Because artists are usually givers and nurturers, but things happen in between. The administrative costs and expenses outweigh the profits, or worse, get "diverted". I am intending these concerts to bypass the pitfalls. It's me and Beau Jarred, maybe Leilah and Jeordie and friends. Johnny Ellis, a lawyer from these parts, helped me when Peter had a heart attack last October. There are only two lawyers out of the hundreds I've been involved with that I would trust with my life, and Johnny Ellis is one of them. He has freely given his time to support our efforts in helping flood victims.

So that's it for now. I haven't played out since, well, November. So I'm terrified, feel unqualified and feel entirely too "woman of size". I think that is the most politically correct way of saying fat, but I'll get over it – I always do.

My dear ones, remember, who knows what's good for you.

# A Big Thank Y'All

*June 27, 2010*

A big heartfelt thank you to all who attended One on One benefit for the Tony Gerber family. It was a great success. Spirits were high and glowing. The vibe in the room was more of a spiritual gathering in some ways than a concert. Up on stage ~ Beau Jarred, firstborn Leilah, as well as grandchildren, Christiana and Aneliese. Musicians from Nashville Tony Gerber, Stevie Ray Anderson from Dr. Hook, Jess Leary. And all the way from the Big A, George Wurzbach on keyboards! Yay...applause, applause. We all appreciate the contribution of The Limelight and crew who donated the night to the event, everything, sound, lights, dressing room amenities and air conditioning. The staff couldn't have been more accommodating and caring,

71

contributing greatly to the atmosphere ~ I could feel their ears.

From the land of a million dreams, it can get hard, so many broken ones. Big cities ~ New York, L.A., where it's all been seen and done ~ that's where I usually do best as far as performing goes, I fall through the cracks of the hard edge. Nashville is different in that music runs through its veins. "Y'all" is the only proper noun, the equivalent of the New York-

New Jersey-Philly "you guys" with a slightly more inclusiveness. Who would have thought this would ever be my home? I recorded one album early in my career, Sunset and Other Beginnings, almost moved here and wrote "Friends and Company" ~ "all I need is some inner peace" but it wasn't time. My New York sensibilities were too intact... Or maybe I knew I'd be too happy here and again it wasn't time. I longed for it but there were things to do, lessons to be learned. I chose the little bit harder way, the road that takes a little longer, but the sites, oh what a sight! We kept moving and now we're all here, full circle, Queens to Nashville but we took the long way. What a road it's been. I'm doing a new Nashville album, 2010, what a sight!

My dear ones, do what I say, not what I do and don't be afraid to know what's good.

*Love, Melanie*

# Let Me Tell You About My Voice

*Author's Note*

"Let me tell you about my voice.
It's big and loud
or tiny and soft.
It comes from several places
In my body and being,
and I truly love it.
I love playing with my voice.
I love using it like thick red paint
or transparent watercolor cerulean blue.
It's certainly not always pretty.
That's not why I give it to you.
There are lots of people
who can give you pretty.
What it is, is, it is me.

And it is very, very important that
you understand~
my voice and I share the same heartbeat.
We cannot be separated by
life, love or death,
just so you know I'm serious about it
and why, if you let my voice in,
we will have a relationship forever.
Of course I am mad." - *Melanie*

# Sugarplums

*December, 2007*

In deference to this political season, I was thinking of canceling Christmahanavaloween this year. Now, a politician is, let's keep this in mind, one who studies what a majority needs or wants and carefully crafts what he says and does to fit those wants and needs. And anything that he has said or done in the past that may contradict his current projected image needs to be convincingly smooth-talked, altered and/or ignored in either a cute cuddly way, or a heart-felt emotional one. ANYTHING. No holds barred, to buy your vote... anything.

So I've taken to looking at what they've actually done and voted for and against, and yes, said, in their past. It's so tempting to go with the "cool" candidate as opposed to the "old fart". Especially us, the Peter Pan generation. I'm pretty sure we half-invented "cool". It's ever so easy to dazzle us with "cool", "in", "now", "hip" and media blah-blah. During election season we need to quit watching television. Just look at the candidates' records. Anyway, remember that voting for the lesser of the two evils is still voting for evil. If you're of the "I don't want to waste my vote" camp, which is kind of silly, as it's a waste either way ~ vote for the least divisive in actions and words. Look at the candidates past and not what they've been cleaned up to be, and on with Christmahanavaloween ~ the season of Peace, Brotherhood and Motherhood of Love.

Chocolate and sugarplums. What are sugarplums? Do Harry and David sell them? If not, why not? Someone could certainly cash in selling sugarplums with a "Ye Olde English" printup of "Twas the Night Before Christmas" poem ~ "While visions of sugarplums danced in their heads". I learned the entire poem when I was three or four. I can hear myself reciting in my high little voice in my head while visions of sugarplums... I remember being stumped by the "As dry leaves before the wild hurricane fly" part, but could recite it anyway. First with my mother prompting me and then by rote. Not until my thirties did I realize the imagery. I cried for all those recitations. Me, capable of that kind of disingenuousness. Imagine being able to pull it off ~ fool people, make them believe what I was saying ~ WOW! There but for fortune I could have been a politician.

My dear ones ~ let's keep up with it. Go with Love. This Christmahanavaloween I am going as Love. What should we wear? Genuine 100% all natural Love. If they ask, what are you supposed to be, don't say a thing. Just have the word displayed in a prominent place and let them feel it. Love, my dear ones, will change the world.

# The Last Great Event

*July 9, 2010*

Isle of Wight, 1970. I flew there on an old army prop plane and had one day to roam down a street in some town, Yarborough I think. I purchased an antique pharmacy jar with voice jujubes written on it. Donovan let me use his gypsy wagon as a backstage dressing room. People camped. The wagon had a coal stove. The fumes were unbearable. The camps everywhere had fires and stoves. I waited and waited. No one wanted to follow The Who. I know Jim Morrison refused. I said, Ok. I think I couldn't stand the fumes any longer and it was so cold. I met the guys from The Who and Keith Moon said he would introduce me. After their amazing set, he did, and handed me his drumstick. I was terrified.

Recently I met Chris Weston, the photographer of "The Last Great Event" (http://www.chrisweston.uk.com) who was with the crew and remembered me going into the sound and light area and crying before I went on. I haven't a memory of that, but I have no reason to doubt it.

Dawn ~ I performed, just me and my guitar, sitting on a low straight back chair. Everyone out there had gone to sleep. It was my job to give them a different dream. As I sang, they awoke, one by one, flowers in the fields. Heads up, standing and cheering at the end. 600,000 of them. I returned to the mainland on hovercraft. On that ride back, with so many kindred spirits, I wrote "The Good Book". A few weeks following my dawning set, I had two top ten albums in England.

Poor little hairy kids out on their own
They run to the festival to show that they were one
They've fallen in love with all human kind
So tell them you love them so they don't change their mind
~ The Good Book


My Dear Ones,

On the stage at the Isle of Wight 2010 I was visited by my angel. I love when that happens! I was singing with the Medina Choir doing the addendum part to Lay Down, (which was created on another stage a few years ago during a different visitation when I added in "Give Peace A Chance" by John Lennon). So now, I am breaking into "all we are saying is give peace a chance... lay down, lay down... and without planning, with complete trust I began the "angel watching over you" chant. The tingle went up my spine and the tears came to the eyes. Not only mine. I think Jimi and John were there. Oh, I hope someday that will happen again, but of course, it won't. Not that particular magic. That was Isle of Wight magic.

"There is a thread that joins each to the other, brother to the sister, sister to the brother"

And then it will be carried on out into the audience (when they get to hear the recording of "Angel Watching Over You") "there is a thread" being sung over "Give Peace a Chance/Lay Down." I know it seems cacophonic, but it works. Of course, it was the angel's idea. So then, we'll have the "thread that joins each to the other, brother to the sister, sister to the brother" taken to other places around the globe. Central Park, NYC. The Mayday Festival in Holland... when will they ever win the soccer World Cup? They always almost get there. I have a great affinity for the Netherlands, as you may know. Some connection for certain. There is a thread... a free festival in London, and so on. There's a thread that joins each to the other.

So the Isle of Wight is fresh and no it wasn't out on the same field. There were Ferris wheels, whirligig rides, people coming for spectacle, performers being shot out of a cannon. Effects and lights. A full blown out NYC skyline erected on stage for Jay-Z. Sir Paul heavily guarded. Barricades. But then, there was just me, making magic, wizard style for Pink and Jay-Z people. Who would have thought it would be me?. What are these angels thinking? I am so grateful for the opportunity to go back to the Isle of Wight. As I think back, I flew home to New York and sat with Jimi Hendrix. It was that trip, his last festival. There are tributes all over the Isle of Wight to Jimi in unlikely places. Outside of the Dimbola Lodge, the historic home of Julia Margaret Cameron, one of the first portrait photographers from the 19th century. John Giddings, a patron for the resurrection of her home (which was almost torn down), and the organizer of the Isle of Wight festival, brought me over and introduced me on stage. No drumstick.

Dr. Brian Hinton, the historian whose guest I was at Dimbola Lodge, the day after the festival, filled me in on Julia Margaret Cameron's life and works. As he led Beau Jarred and I through her rooms and walls filled with her portraits, there in this nearly demolished and now restored jewel, I met Guy Portelli, the sculptor, who's done a Jimi Hendrix and is now going to be doing a Melanie. I am honored. We sat and had the most amazing cakes and tea in the teahouse part of the lodge.

Roadburn Cafe was born out of a want to share some road stories and talk about the unique food experiences. I think the first entry had to do with Tim Horton's Donuts, so now I'll bring it all home with the cakes. The sponges, the cremes and bumble-berry tarts, oh here's the menu. To sit in this lovely tearoom with the dedicated group, dedicated to what? A higher ground. A refuge to some. Works in progress. The dreams of artists, authentic lives. Looking out onto the garden where a bronze of Jimi Hendrix stands, head down, guitar in hand. If he were here, we'd be having tea and cakes and wondering, what is time and where does it go? And maybe we would come up with a song about the last great event, or the one to come. Beau could tell him, and perhaps show him his new guitar technique. Maybe we would just sip tea and eat cakes before posing in front of the statue. Wipe crumbs off our faces before Charles Everest or Chris Weston snapped us 40 years on. My dear ones still.

With life, love and dreams,
Melanie

P.S. Thank you to Eve Cook who made it all happen, and schlepped us everywhere along the tiny roads along the Isle of Wight. Thanks to the Dimbola Lodge teahouse staff for the cakes and hospitality, to the intensely enthusiastic Brian, to Guy and Chris, the innkeepers at Frenchman's Cove, to Susan and Chris for putting up with our crazy schedule and making us full English breakfast at 13:00 and making us feel at home. The Medina Choir and choir director Hannah Redman who helped bring on the angels. And finally to John Giddings for inviting me to the 40th anniversary of the last great event.

# Rambling and Meambling

*September 1st, 2010*

A stop along the way at the Roadburn Cafe.

My dear ones, I've learned to trust myself more than others might. Every time I've ignored that little voice, the one that tells me beyond all reason why I should or shouldn't, there's been trouble. I listened when I was 20 teen something, but then later when I became 30 ten 2, I figured adulthood. Make adult decisions based on what a responsible grownup person would do. Be more like this one or that one, other mothers, perceptions of maturity, Joan Baez or Christine Amanpour NORMAL. I was touring in England and met a world renowned psychic who told me the stress of trying to be normal was making me crazy. Boy did that hit the mark. Where was Melanie? Who was Melanie? At first, Melanie was an outcast, oddball, didn't measure up to my family's expectations, a runaway, thrown out of school to become a superstar with golden records and silver chains and glass chains and new ideas about who I should be, further removed from who I was. It's very difficult to look for yourself with so many others looking for you. Somewhere in there was my personal owness, the authentic me, real, the genuine article, not what I was called, labeled, built up or torn down to be, not the one who was applauded or discarded later.

We are all going to die.
You will die.
I will die and what was that?
What was that called my life? I wanted to be of service to mankind, to humanity, I have a love for humanity which pales sometimes by my fear of the one on one because I have it seems pulled in, or my position, perhaps would draw in the ones who want to see if they can make you cry.

"I cried out loud but they didn't understand. I cried so hard I may never cry again."
(I Am Not a Poet)

I recently looked at my performances on the Ed Sullivan show, Wow! I was really good and so pretty. I was unaware of that at the time it's true. And so what, even if I was aware of it, that isn't the point. It's this human condition. From the most optimistic viewpoint, life is a beautiful chance. A possibility of

the unlimited possible. A fulfillment of creation giving birth to all creations. All art, music, love and ultimately death. From the less optimistic viewpoint, it's suffering, or falling in step with the banal dance, the insipid false laughter, busy work. The moves one makes to succeed in business, social standing to find money, power, sex, degradation, loneliness, sorrow and ultimately death. We're all gonna die!
I don't wanna, but it's the deal, the sacred contract. So I'm going to follow this through to the end and beyond ~Bed, Bath and further than that.

The little voice that has no voice, said, so call the new CD, "Ever Since You Never Heard of Me". The loud mouth said "It's too long." You should call it "Tried to Die Young." One of the best songs on it. Or something more intellectual, something Leonard Cohen would be proud of. I don't know if Leonard is ever proud. It's an unintellectual word. Pride, in Roget's Thesaurus is a sense of self worth, self respect, self esteem, but the symptoms of pride listed go on and on from arrogance, condescension, vain glory, airs, boasting, conceit, chauvinistic, too big for one's boots. Of course, who would be caught dead being proud, but I'm defensive of proud. Probably, because it was beaten out of me early on and I've fought for it. Look, just summon up that feeling of being proud.

OK Now here we go

just summon up that feeling of being proud..........

Do you feel condescending, too big for your boots or arrogant? Well not me. I feel really good. It's nice up here. Ooooohhh I'm proud. Ooooh put that on once a day and you probably won't kill yourself or you could go to Bacoma, Oklahoma, if you touch the ground there you won't suicide yourself says Edgar Cayce. Why bother? If any of the spiritual practices are even a little right, it's no way to beat the system. "We're going on a bear hunt, we're going to catch a big one. What a beautiful day. We're not scared, can't go under it. Can't go over it. Oh no, we've got to go through it." So here it is ESYNHOM in its entirety with only bits left out. "Will you still please me, will you still need me, When I'm sixty-four. You'll be older too." In my 64th year, but not yet 64 and in the spirit of how old would you be if you didn't know how old you were ~ about 23, 42, something in there. An archaeologist, a member of the Peace Corps, next life, or in heaven I'll save you all a chair, my dear ones. Thank for listening and don't read anything into this, I've already done it for you,

Love
Melanie


The Loudmouth: Better read this over. I don't know about this telling people they're gonna die stuff or Leonard Cohen not being proud or killing yourself and sex and degradation?

Little Voice: I know but this is true from my little voice place of importance.
Sorry but I win!

# The Last Tale from the Roadburn Café

*November 22, 2010*

My Dear Ones,

"Melanie, I love you. I would give up my life for you."
"Why Peter, why do you always say that?"
"Because it is true."
And we would both know that <u>right there,</u> where others might think of it as aberrated, over the top, crazy beyond crazy love, it was true. I have a larger-than-life story to tell so this last journal entry might be shorter or longer - will be, could be different. Of course, one never knows really. I'll read it over later and tell you if you'll ever see it.

Peter, my husband of 45 years, partner, friend, father of our children left his body behind on this Working Legend Tour. He dropped me off at a Whole Foods in Framingham, Massachusetts, said he'd be back, had to get a new phone at Best Buy. Now we're checked into our hotel, Beau Jarred was in the room, one of those home-away-from-home places. As we were going to be there for the week, I was stocking up. I had gone down all the aisles two times and putting more into the cart that we could ever use in a week and then I thought, "celery", and "oh, these are local apples" -it was night and the store was getting ready to close. I sat at the café part and had one of the containers of soup that I had gotten us for dinner -I waited and waited and when no message came, I knew it must be from you. I grew uneasy, wavering between anger and nagging fear - where is he? I'll wait outside - With my overloaded cart, I went out and sat on a haystack. They were all decked-out out front, pumpkins and mums. The service manager asked if I needed help or something and I used her phone to call Peter. It went right to voicemail. Peter where are you? A man walked across the parking lot, no, that's not him. Another car like ours, then no it's not. Then two police cars pulled up - why two police cars? Nothing bad is happening at Whole Foods..."Are you Melanie Schekeryk?" "Is he all right?" I knew. "No," the policeman replied - I think he was experienced in this.

I kept crying, No, no, it's not possible ~ the police said "my son was being picked up to go to the hospital." Beau was in the hotel room alone expecting our call when he was told by a doctor. I went into the police car backseat alone, the grate in the middle, my heart in hand cuffs and I thought, maybe it's not true, maybe it's a mistake. I went into the hospital and Beau was brought from the other direction and there was the old Peter the Great. His shell, the energy container, he was nowhere to be seen or felt. He had a soft, self-satisfied expression on his face, almost a smile. We left our kisses on this remnant of himself ~ trying to contact ~ and we did back at the hotel in the trees and wind outside, the autumn leaves speaking in colors through my soul.     But Peter has left the building, no mistake ~ He won't be picking me up anymore.

The man who was helping him with the phone at Best Buy came to our hotel room the next day. We hugged and cried. He told me of Peter's last words ~ Peter was my biggest fan, ardent admirer~

I'm sorry... wait, I can't, yes I can~

I was his only client from the day he met me. The Best Buy salesman said he was telling him all about me, promoting me at Best Buy. "Peter, you nut" ~ He leaned on the counter, said, "I don't feel very well." The kid gave him water and Peter proceeded to tell him how I started the lighting of things at concerts, because of the event at Woodstock. "It was Melanie," were his last words as they helped him down and called the paramedics but he was gone. I waited and when no message came, I knew it was from you.

Two nights later, Beau and I did the scheduled show. They said I could cancel but Peter said "No." It was a great night and Peter was there and always will be. I will continue this life... Peter won't have it any other way. So many of you who knew us sent condolences and prayers and a flow of love that you might want some of the details ~ the last tale from the Roadburn Café ~ We all die. You'd think they would start our first days of preschool with "Good Morning, children you were born and someday you will be unborn. Get to know who you are and love everyone because we are all in this together." But as it is, death is shunned, put behind the doors, "it happens to other people" "He was in a high stress profession, I'm a librarian." "I stop work at 5 o'clock and leave it in the office." "Not so, even calm peaceful ones will expire and do what we came here to do." ~life, death, life ~

 So Peter wanted me to write a book and I never could start or rather, I could start and never continue. He even brought a bright leather bound book so I could.
 "Melanie, I love you. I would give up my life for you. Write it, Melanie, please, I love the way you write."

 I never saw it was Peter who was the story, the book. It will be Peter's story, immigrant refugee to number one producer of Melanie, the love of his life. That crazy Peter, sometimes you can't see it's a story till it ends, the greatest love story never told. I have a lot to do, my dear ones. Please hold my hand tonight. Love, Melanie

*Love Melanie*

83

# Out of Towner

Tiny shiny small
and briney
Slivers tossed by seaside shore
I'll only take the broken bits today
And nothing more

Nothing more
I'll leave the best for tourists
I was once a tourist so I understand
They see me pass over a good one
And then swoop down and swipe the sand
I smile at the game I play with
The foreigners
Tomorrow they can be the local
I'll be the out-of-towner

Rough and tumbled
cracked and crumbled
Slivers colored shards and rubble
Tomorrow you can be the local
Me, the out-of-towner

# P.S.
## It Comes in Waves

*October 1, 2011*

It has been almost one year since Peter the Great went missing. And it comes in waves. They roll in and I'm under and cannot recover. Scraping along the gravel shell bottom of the sea. Which way is up? I become a ball of downward momentum with appendages and finally dizzy but still breathing. "So sorry for your loss" coming less and less. People know I've been to that place where no one wants to go. It's uncomfortable, dangerous and perhaps contagious. I know, I was there. Not knowing what to say. Now that the immediacy is gone, they think it went away. They don't see the clinging shards and rubble from my bout with the wave. Nor do they detect my gasping for air. Most think, "Why remind her? Why bring it up?" That's how I felt before, before "denile"...a river in Egypt. Ignore it and it still flows into the great sea where I was knocked off my feet, spun round senseless, broken and still barely catching a breath. Smiling, joking, living...the great tribute to human survival.

October 26, 2010, a one year memorial. I will play "Beautiful People", a song Peter produced, risking his job with CBS by telling it them it was just a demo session and booking a full-out union string session with Harry Lakowski. John Abbott was the arranger. And me singing in one take as Peter was so fond of saying, "she did it all in one take." The tears of joy came later as I was swept away with the music, all of that counterpoint and a line I had hummed becoming a counter melody. My song living its own life. I was giving birth and Peter was the birthing coach. CBS knew nothing of it until the bills came in...and it was too late. Studio techs in white lab coats! Far away behind the glass, Peter in the middle of the room gesturing wildly, a conductor from Hell making sure everyone in the room could see and feel me: no vocal booth. And we make our first recording together at last, for the first time.

October 26th, at 9 PM (Eastern), we'll play "Beautiful People". Join me.

# My Initial Thoughts

*June 11, 2011*

England is coming...and I'm going to England. Leaving from the USA, and going to the UK. I feel the powers that be are making a case for initials. It seems less personal...less of a country and more of a brand. Like KFC, BMW, BOA, AMC and IBM.

Initials and text speak and "LOL"... that's the first time I've actually written LOL. Face-to-face, or at least on the phone, that's my preference. There are inflections, things that hang in the air, sincerity or insincerity ~ Real.

I think that 2012 will herald in Real. Everyone who isn't will have to go from England to the UK, from America to the US.

See you real soon...for real.

Love,
Melanie

Am I Real Or What?

# The Scorpions
# Are Coming

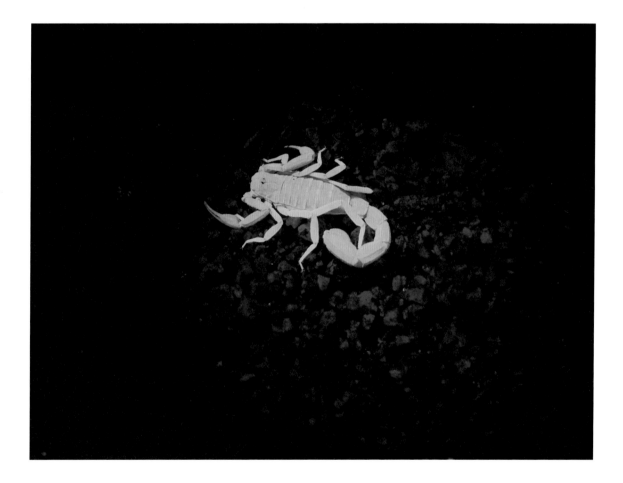

June 18, 2011

My Dear Ones,

I am in the desert with Beau. The scorpions are coming.

We drove across the country from Massachusetts to Arizona after Peter left his body on October 26, 2010. He had booked several shows in the Northeast, one in Massachusetts. And only a few days after he was no longer here, Beau and I felt compelled to finish up the gigs Peter had scheduled.

Beau never drove before. Beau was always the "artist in residence" passenger in the back seat of the car, or in the air. So it was all strange and other worldly to be going to Arizona by car. But we had planned it that way and that is the way we did it. You might or might not know I don't drive ~ I have a license (and a perfect driving record), I just don't use it. I'm a New Yorker. And then I became famous and was always driven and delivered. It was never my job or Beau's to transport.

So the last stop for us was Arizona, the desert part. The saguaros, Highway 101 to the 202 to 60 and so on. Not the LIE to the Cross Bronx. All the water here is driven and delivered.

No, we've not been home to Nashville. We were taken in, first by friends of Jeordie. Jeordie has lived here for 10 years. Jeordie writes, sings and plays out 4 to 5 days a week in the Phoenix area. I so far can't face going back to what was home...Leilah, Christiana, Analisa.

I met a remarkable woman who hosts shows at the New Vision Church, picks fruit for the homeless, does Bikram yoga, is a high roller at the casinos in Las Vegas and wins. She owns an upscale consignment shop all around the theme of *The Wizard of Oz*, is a champion for LGBT causes and lives what people think of as the 60s ideals. She opened the door of her home and gave Beau and I a place to heal. Peter is saving her a chair in heaven. Beau wrote her a piece of music and me ~ when I get well again will think of a way.

Right now, the angels are having their way with me. Sometimes I am alone in this world, an inhabitant of an Ursula Le Guin novel ~ I rage, I cry ~ then it is as if nothing is different and I am OK, and then not ~ and we persist through this unimaginable, through the waves ~ or, as the line from my new song *Live One* goes, "is it brave or just the will to drown".

I'm in the desert. The scorpions are coming.

Love,  Melanie

# Glastonbury and
# A Leap of Faith

*June 27, 2011*

*My Dear Ones,*

It's England, I'm here, Glastonbury ~ so were so many of you. All standing through the downpour in ankle deep mud, (Woodstock! What is it this thing with mud and festivals?) listening.

From my vantage point, the tops of glistening heads and umbrellas ~ crowds as far as I can see, mouthing the words to my songs, even the new ones ~ how grateful I am to be able to sing and create for so many receptive people all over the world.

From the rain and the mud to fine theatres, auditoriums, city or town centers ~ likely and unlikely places, clubs (Ronnie Scotts, Union Chapel in Islington, Canterbury Cathedral after that.) But now Glastonbury. Back lights playing the rain double time ~ Kamikaze rain.

It went too fast for all the build-up beginning last year in October when Peter went away. Time went on, but then...

| | |
|---|---|
| Person: | Are you doing Glastonbury? |
| Melanie: | I don't know... |
| Another Person: | I heard you're doing Glastonbury. It's the biggest festival in Europe. |
| Melanie: | It's not for sure, lots of details are unclear |
| Voice in Melanie's Head: | Melanie, go to Glastonbury |
| Angel Voice: | You'll go ~ one more leap of faith |

Then I remember, Melanie remembers, Peter promising to be there.

| | |
|---|---|
| Glastonbury People: | We need an answer. We need to know if you're doing Glastonbury. We need to know today. |

I knew I had to go, no matter what. Even though circumstances were uncertain ~ one more leap of faith.

We glop through the mud and past the "Pyramid" stage and onto the "Spirit of '71". The spirit is up there where I'm supposed to be. I let it go, the disappointments, the loss, I let it go. I'm a professional :)

I stand under a make shift canopy for a BBC interview. The hem of my Bedouin wedding dress sinking lower into the mud.

| | |
|---|---|
| Interviewer Clair: | So this is a rather emotional performance for you? |
| Melanie: | Yes, it's been a long road since 1971. Peter, the producer of all those songs ~ that soundtrack lives, comes back again and again in different incarnations, nostalgia to some, new songs to children ~ is no longer in this body form. He promised to be here with me at this year's Glastonbury, and he is. |
| | Knowing him, he'll be bouncing around from me to Bare Naked Ladies and U2. He always loved artists. (Let me tell you some time about how he wanted to sign Bruce Springsteen and I wouldn't let him.) |
| | Andrew Kerr, the father of Glastonbury, greeted me as I arrived. We shared moments and memories of us, all three at the farm house...he, Peter and I as we set about to be part of making this world a better place. There is a beautiful sadness and a great power here. |
| | Yes Claudia, it will be an emotional performance. I wasn't sure I would go through with it. But I got the go ahead from a very high place. |

Yes, it's been a long road since '71 till now. Peter would always say, "Melanie, you don't know who you are." ~ My dear ones ~ I'm learning.

Love, Melanie

# Peanut Butter & Feathers

*August 4, 2011*

My Dear Ones,

England is now Chicago and I'm in the same suitcase. I shift things around so the bags don't weigh too much, but they still do ~ they make these large suitcases to be filled only with feathers. If you fill them with clothing, shoes, socks, undies, accessories and cosmetics...all the things you cannot carry on (Beau brings peanut butter, one jar for emergencies. I bring Tuna Panang from Trader Joe's)...your bag will be overweight. Cars are made to go over a hundred miles an hour when we can only go sixty...and suitcases are destined to be overweight and people penalized by the unscrupulous airlines. Oh yes, "the price of gas", I know, I know. And "the freeze in Florida", so that citrus that was picked before the freeze is three times as much anyway.

I have begun to travel with feathers only, and why couldn't I be more like Christiane Amanpour? She travels only with a trench coat...a trench coat and she uses hotel amenities...and Bill Clinton who berated her in front of the world for asking an impertinent question and she didn't flinch. She didn't stand down. I probably would have cried. Though I'd have tried not to, as soon as that lower lip started to quiver, boing! (Eye makeup and all...that heavy makeup bag.) It all comes down to that or I'd be able to stand up to bullying.

So it's feathers only from now on.


Love,
Melanie

93

# Healing the Enemy

*August 11, 2011*

*My Dear Ones,*

Who needs book burning?

It's 7 a.m., I'm on British time and I'm in Chicago.

I'm the guest of Larry Garrett, the author of <u>Healing the Enemy</u>. Talk about people with a story not aligned with the current political agenda.

Oprah ~ Larry King ~ yoohoo...who needs book burning or the banning of certain music that doesn't conform when the powers that be have the 3 Ms: marketing, manipulation technology and money to force the undesirables into obscurity ~ Oh my dear ones, I'm only joking. Or is it my keen sense of observation was having a public moment? "Down, down!"

Onto love and light. Got to keep the love and light. It's the only way.

Love,
Melanie

# The Grande Dame of Woodstock

*August 7, 2011*

My Dear Ones,

It's been a while ~ I am not celebrity material ~ I am an artist, impeccable according to my own standard. But fame, vain glory, celebrity, I'm just not so good at that. It probably comes from my leftist, union-organizing, never show "the wheat that grows highest is always cut down" upbringing. There was, however, a chink in all of that -- my father. My father the capitalist who drove, of all things, a Caddy or a Buick convertible. Not a Ford or a VW. So somewhere in my deepest self is the wheat woman who would be cut down driving a Caddy. But of course, "I ride my bike, I rollerskate, don't drive no car".

I walked into a restaurant, Pita Jungle and just happened to sit next to the owner. Now this is a fast food, healthy, Mediterranean establishment--well known in Arizona--that is truly amazing in its blending: cross-ethnic, fire-roasted chipotle with tahini sauces blending, blending sesame-oriental, infused with something unmistakably Italian. Over-the-top I am about this place, you just cannot get sick of it. There is the garlic dip and if you don't want carbs (pita bread) with your dips and hummus, they'll slice up fresh cucumbers for you. Not the ones that have been sliced and sitting in ice, but fresh-sliced. So I was almost crying because Peter (you know him, but maybe you do) who just recently passed away, would have by now been best friends with the owner sitting next to us ~ but Peter wasn't there.

95

Or was he?

The wheat woman driving a Caddy, as she was leaving, introduced herself. The proprietor was sitting with perhaps investors and their wives...and me, the most unassuming of all, the unlikeliest candidate for celebrity, walked over to the assembled and announced, "Your food is so special that I want you have my new album. I am Melanie."

Peter was so proud as I walked out into the night and opened the door of my Caddy. Beau Jarred closed the door behind the Grande Dame of Woodstock and wheat stalks went flying down the 101 South.

Love,

Melanie

# Movin' On Up

*August 23, 2011*

My Dear Ones,

I am on the 58th floor of the John Hancock Building on Michigan Avenue. A magazine of that same name ~ with a photo of Jennifer Hudson, her new body, her new look, her new marriage ~ lies on the cushion of the window seat that spans the length of the living room overlooking Lake Michigan, Sears Tower (I still call it "Sears Tower"), and countless architectural wonders.

Another thirty-six floors up is the observation tower ~ people line up in droves to see what I am seeing from a little higher up. I sit on the window seat and look out onto Oprah's penthouse ~ and right here some of you might be thinking, Wow!

But on this particular night, we will make do with just a few bare essentials because this luxurious apartment is also completely unfurnished. Beau and I share our leftover Uno's pizza from the night before, the Spinacoli, which is cheese, spinach, broccoli and sauce. Sitting on two folding chairs and using another two bar stools for our plates, we light a candle and eat our dinner while we watch the fireworks display over Navy Pier. Beau takes lots of photos ~ I've never seen fireworks from above.

We finish the pizza, drink up our Barq's root beer and then dump the paper plates and crumbs into the grocery shopping bag we've been using for trash and wash the plastic utensils. We find a discarded lamp when we throw out the trash, off the hallway, that works! We review the photos, we inflate our blow-up beds, and the shower behind the discount bin shower curtain liner. (Lucky for us, I collect hotel amenities.) We crawl under our borrowed bedding and we say a prayer for our unknown host. She is a friend of a friend of a friend.

My life, my life, the story of my life is much too long and complicated and most of it untrue. My Dear Ones, furnished or not, welcome to the lifestyles of the rich and famous.

Love from the Squatters on the 58th floor.

Melanie

# It Boils Down to This

*October 11, 2011*

My Dear Ones,

It boils down to <u>this.</u> And I'm always looking for that <u>this.</u>
"Oh how simplistic, Melanie," you say.
But there must be an underlying cause for war, inhumanity, cruel behavior,
sometimes disguised as "those are the rules".
Crazy laws get put into place, turning perfectly nice people into criminals
and other nice people into enforcers of law.
Because mankind is good, it must boil down to a terrible <u>this.</u>
<u>This</u> is on the tip of my tongue or
wedged into that part of my brain that has
been turned off somewhere along the line.
Ever since I've found out that dormant other has been freeloading,
it's been a highly suspect candidate for <u>this.</u>

Another bone of contention is intestines.
More nooks and crannies, twists and turns,
predisposed to all kinds of problems ~ next time someone is going to design a race,
the colon and intestines,
take a better look in that area.
I don't pretend to know, I'm just pointing out built-in potential for trouble
so a brilliant, good person can correct the basic design flaws,
deliberately built in or mistakes.
And please, flying.
I know how it feels, don't you?
How could we possibly ever know if we've never done it?
If I were going to submit new design plans,
I would bring back flying.
"Please don't try <u>this</u> at home."

Love,
Melanie

# Christmas Is Here

*December 18, 2011*

"Christmas, oh Christmas, Christmas is here;
Everyone will give a great big cheer.
The children are happy, the children are gay;
Hooray, hooray for Christmas Day!"

This is the first thing I composed that was printed in the PS5 first or second grade section of the school paper, and in fact was the first time I remember seeing my name in print. Melanie Safka. I was just learning to read and it's bizarre that I just remembered it. I suppose because Christmas is coming and I'm watching my wild animal. I'm living with a cat-toon. Jeordie caught her for me. To have a companion in my grief, she presented the beast in a parking lot on my birthday. I call her "Moo shu" as people were already calling her "the little pork nugget". So the first thing that came to mind was "Moo shu" as in moo shu pork.

Her full name is Moo shu, Pork Nugget II. The second because I suspect there have been other pork nuggets. Moo shu is not all cat. She is all over brownish with hints of red and black highlights or lowlights. The tail is short and raccoon shaped; legs short, paws huge for her size. She is small and long haired, not a big fluff ball cat. But with pronounced mane, her fur is not exactly soft, more bear like. Several black lines on her face are the source of great amusement. I know it's not nice to laugh at others but there is this crooked black marking line on her mouth giving her ridiculousness in her regal cat face. A Billy Idol sort of sneer, greenish eyes with black eyeliner, and at least 10 definite expressions, and twice that in body language. Oh, and she scurries like a rodent, but then changes back to catwalk elegance. When she sits upright, she is an ancient Egyptian with a long neck and pronounced arch in the back. She is vampire too, so trendy these days. She will not be seen and finds the darkest recesses by day and appears only after dark. Not exactly a comforting cozy lap thing, but when she's certain I'm down, she'll slither onto the bed and sleep there all night and lets me touch her. As soon as I'm up, she's the wild thing once more.

She's looking at me now...and at invisible beings out of our dimension. Ears going back and forth like antennas honing into a signal like me. Only my ears don't move. She'll be heading for the closet as soon as I begin my day just a few weeks before Christmas.

Pretty soon I will have a manager, or rather, two managers. I've never had a manager before, I've always managed. And when people asked, I would say Peter, because there wasn't anyone else. Manager puts me in mind of a boxer. "Get him kid!" My eyes focused on invisible beings and listening for signals, poised and waiting to pounce. Maybe I'm spending too much time with my cat. Managers will get me out of that. I'll be on the road soon, I'll be in your face, that's what we hope. NOT me of course, I don't really want to be in your face, it's just part of the job, now more than ever. I became invisible sometime in the 80s. I didn't do anything, it just happened. People give pretend reasons, but it's stuff and nonsense really. I just became invisible. I keep singing, keep writing, putting music out. Yes, I have a website and my half-assed Facebook. (I'm sorry, but I am not going to spend my days and nights chit-chatting. I'm creating or recovering or both. I love you all, My Dear Ones, but I don't "check in" too much.) Maybe managers will help. They are Doug Yeager and David Wilkes. Their new joint venture is me, in your face, get him kid. Invisible me, a woman with a past, or should I say a history? What do I do, what do I go as? The hippie Susan Boyle? Both my cat and I don't mind you laughing at us, as long as it's a good laugh.

Merry Christmas.

Love,
Melanie

# The Ministry of Keep Breathing

*December 21, 2011*

So the truth is it's not getting better. The intensity and dynamics of this grief are different and better in that I am functioning on a day to day sort of way with inner life pushed to one side in the obvious ways. (No crying in stores, at public gatherings or on the street.)

For a woman who's given birth, it's like a contraction, a big one. Hitting all at once, out of nowhere ~ you're breathing, perhaps Lamaze breathing ~ you've just had a whopper and you're breathing. It should be a minute or two until the next one but then, Bang and two in a row with no recovery time, nothing to prepare you ~ I go off to the market. I'll eat lunch. I will watch Brenda Watson on PBS...The Road to Perfect Health. I need to be a supporter of PBS. Somewhere in the back of my mind, Peter should have been taking Probiotics. We both knew Brenda Watson in Florida. I've become a PBS supporter. Why didn't we get on a better health regimen? I go to bed with slight regret. Sleep all night, too. All night. Wake a bit too early, can't catch my breath...complete panic. It's the big one, one more push. This is too much, give me drugs. Breathe through it. No, it's not possible. The policeman says, "Yes, he's dead." No, I'm supposed to die first. You've made a mistake. "No", he says.

It's now a year later, and again and again with unbearable force, coupled with irrational thoughts and I keep breathing. No birth. That baby is still in there. I'll just keep breathing. One more cleansing breath. Now I ask myself, is this appropriate? Should anyone out there see it? I'm sorry if anyone thinks not. It's all I can do. This and breathing. Just breathe. The telephone rings. Yes? Oh, a walk? A walk would be nice. Even though I prefer to walk with a dog, I don't have one. Cats won't. I do have 3 strange little creatures and I apologize for all the analogies in this past year, in this last year's entries. All the sorrow I might have unleashed on you, My Dear Ones. But this is a big one and it lives, and isn't going away. It seems one hell of a payoff but then I've never believed in payoffs. And I keep writing it down because that is how I figure things out. Otherwise thoughts just short-circuit, don't go anywhere, never resolve. But if I were a really good writer, I would resolve everything and then perhaps start my own religion. There must be loads of folks like me...in and out of funk and grief. Any answer might be better than none at all. Maybe between the lines, here and there, is an answer. The obvious one is keep breathing.

My Dear Ones, join me in my Ministry of Keep Breathing.

Love,
Melanie

# Agitated

"Before I go on I get so agitated, so nervous.
It's like I have to go into a hostile atmosphere of thick light, blackness and smoke, where I need a different breathing apparatus,
a gill or a new hole in my head.
Then I am there ~ and it is more natural on stage than in the other place.
(You see, I must already have that extra hole in my head.)
I make the transformation, and while everybody's watching.
Then I am there ~ and it is my world.
I am swimming and floating, flying, diving and sometimes running for my life.
Then it is ninety minutes ~ it's over and I think 'just a few more.'
And I have to go back to the place that was so hard for me to leave:
Real life.
I cover up that hole in my head and tuck in the gill till next time. "

# The Hands

There are ways of making lace
no Belgian woman could or can.
There are corporate cakes
and machines that make
an almost sun kissed tan.
And though they're nearly breathing
Perfect, life-like, better than -
There are mistakes a human makes.
But there's something about the hands.

107

# Along the well worn verboten path

Along the well worn verboten path
Amongst the safer russet roofs I fly
behind the dream
with broken promises
and tear stained face
I may be gone
But gone is not a place

# In Closing

In my early teens while reading *The Diary of Anne Frank,* I came upon her words "I still believe people are good." And right there I wept, as I reconnected with a soul mate, and my path appeared.

It was a beautiful sadness, embracing the ideals of a family of man. I knew we were here to help each other ~ Anne Frank helped me there, beyond time, space and physical presence in this universe.

I dedicated myself to be of service to man.

Armed with these lofty ideals I spent the next 20 or so years figuring out just how to do that.

During that time, I, with much protest on my part, became a celebrity, a first name only star.

My purpose, seemingly, and to my own disappointment, being shoved behind a closing door.

However living in a peopled world I was, beyond knowing, affecting ~ having an effect, and my purpose was pulling in after *Woodstock, Beautiful People, Lay Down,* audiences who would always break down the barriers.

My unspoken invitation rang clear that we needed to get "close to it all", realize our connectiveness and support one another as we are all in this together, and whether or not you are having fun, there are vast others who are not, and we need to do something about that.

The gathering around me wasn't so much a kitsch "thing to do." It was real, make no mistake. Ed Sullivan himself knew it was a magic moment and allowed it to happen, and happen it did on his show. He told Peter that this was something truly unique and authentic that was unfolding, and he would not stop it.

Peter was moved to the point of giving Ed a ring I had given Peter! A bit of a sore point, but understandable.

*Brand New Key,* yes The Roller Skate Song, was the kiss of death to my future as the Mother Teresa of Rock. My public image along that line thwarted ~ people are so silly, adorable, but easily swayed by the machinery of fame. It wasn't important to me. I kept at it without knowing or caring as I wandered the planet for UNICEF, singing at the General Assembly and under the Angel of Peace.

And on two different occasions at the DMZ border in South Korea, I performed where mementos of love, peace flags, garments of loved ones who were separated by that barren three-mile terrible divide ~ my voice carrying north. There I was unexpectedly named "honorary ambassador of peace to South Korea."

So I continued through all these years with "Tales from the Roadburn Café."

I meet lots of ones who gathered and once sat around me, and many new "born again hippies" who will bring along a line or song that got them through ~ sometimes we cry. And I am affirmed that I indeed am doing what I set out to do.

Some of the vintage ones will ask in that shell-shocked sort of way ~ "Melanie, what happened? Where did it all go?"

It's here, I say. Maybe in Occupy Wall Street. Not in a force, but in a power that lives and grows. People will rise to a cause... And I still believe people are good.

And we will give out all our peaches and prunes And I shall be proud of my wisteria blooms Oh row upon row of your favorites soon In the house of the sweet perfume They'll be space for a slide And a swing and you'll ride A two-wheeler down the drive Or fly 'cross a cable attached to the moon In the house of the sweet perfume And I know you'll grow strong And be ready for anything And be there for your brothers and sisters and friends And we'll all have our own room We can scream or loud sing His or her own tune And every night dancing With mop handles and brooms In the house of the sweet perfume You'll lie under feathers In your very own room In the house of the sweet perfume The walls will be thick We'll be there for your brothers and sisters and friends

CPSIA information can be obtained
at www.ICGtesting.com
Printed in the USA
LVXC02n1320071214
417625LV00028B/93